H

 W9-AQZ-845

GIVEN BY
FRIENDS OF
CHEROKEE COUNTY
PUBLIC LIBRARIES

GIVE THE DOG A BONE

STEVEN KELLOGG

SeaStar Books

New York

Boppity BAM!
For Arlen and Sam.
Nickity NACK!
For Peter and Zack.

Copyright © 2000 by Steven Kellogg

SEASTAR BOOKS
a division of NORTH-SOUTH BOOKS, INC.

First published in the United States by SeaStar Books, a division of North-South Books, Inc., New York.
Published simultaneously in Great Britain, Canada, Australia, and New Zealand by North-South Books,
an imprint of Nord-Süd Verlag AG, Gossau Zürich, Switzerland.

Library of Congress Cataloging-in-Publication Data is available.
A CIP catalogue record for this book is available from The British Library.

The art for this book was prepared using a combination of colored ink, watercolor, acrylic, and colored pencil.
The text for this book is set in Kennerly, Windsor, and Bostonian.
Designed by Judythe Sieck

ISBN 1-58717-001-9 (trade binding)
1 3 5 7 9 TB 10 8 6 4 2
ISBN 1-58717-002-7 (library binding)
1 3 5 7 9 LB 10 8 6 4 2

Printed by Proost NV in Belgium

For more information about our books, and the authors and artists who create them,
visit our web site: www.northsouth.com

This old man, he played ONE,
He played nick-nack on his drum.

Nickity Nackity
Nackity Nickity
Nickity Nackity
Nackity Nickity
Nickity
Nackity
NACK!

Nick-nack paddywhack, give the dog a bone,
This old man went rolling home.

This old man, he played **TWO**,
He played nick-nack on his shoe.

Nick-nack paddywhack, give the dogs a bone,

This old man went cobbling home.

This old man, he played THREE,

Nick-nack-nick and . . .

Up the tree!

Nick-nack paddywhack, give the dogs a bone,

This old man went purring home.

This old man, he played FOUR,
Nick-KNOCK, Nick-KNOCK on the door.
KNOCK-nack, paddywhack...

Would you like a BONE?

This old man was welcomed home.

Toss the dogs a bone,

This old man hightailed it home.

This old man, he played SIX,
Told the hen to hatch six chicks...

Nick-nack paddywhack, took the chickies home,

This old man, he played SEVEN,
Soared right up to doggy heaven.

Nick-nack paddywhack, served them all a bone,

Good-bye kisses,

Sailed back home.

This old man, he played EIGHT,

Past his bedtime,
much too late.

Nick-nack paddywhack,

Eight kind sled dogs hauled him home.

This old man, he played NINE,
Playing nick-nack, feeling fine.

Nick-nack paddywhack, when the ball was thrown,
This old man went sliding home.

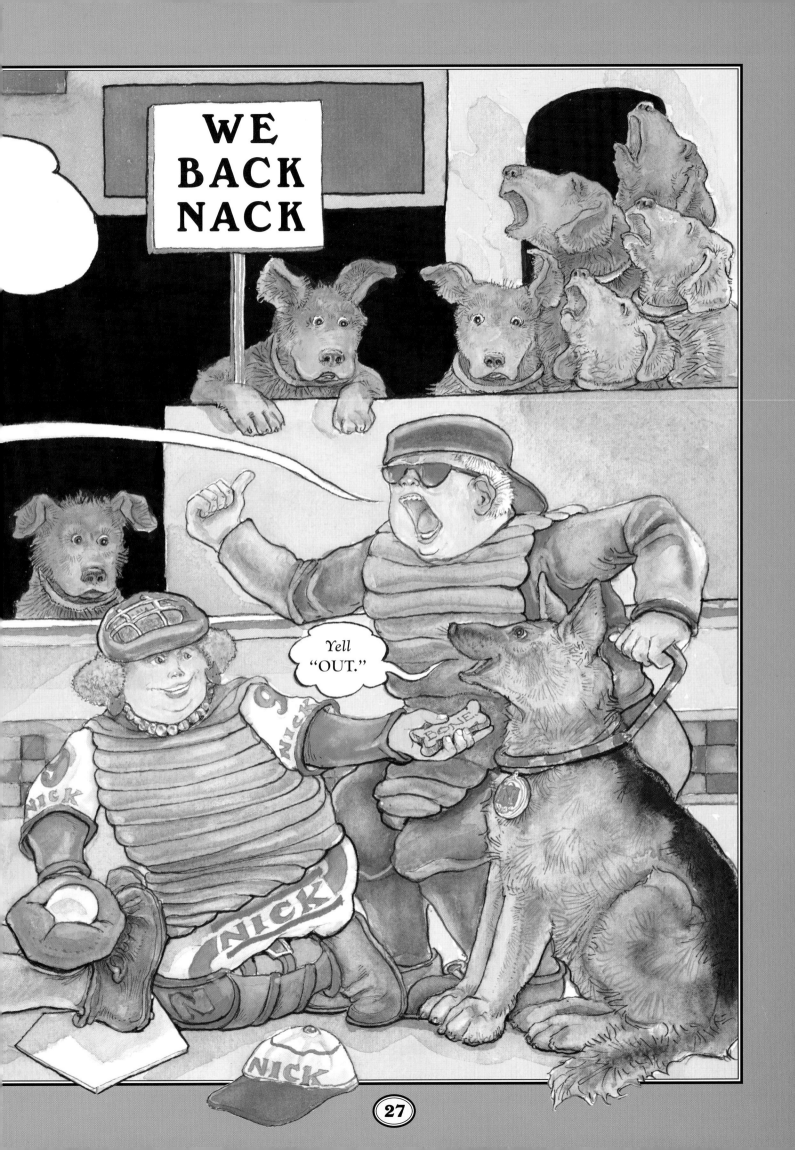

Nick-nack, shells crack,

Raptors want a bone…

Grabbed their bones and raptored home.

🦴 A NOTE ABOUT THE SONG 🦴

This Old Man is a popular nonsense counting song of uncertain origin (perhaps English, perhaps American) that seems to have first appeared in the early twentieth century. Hundreds of variations can be found, since improvisation is often the most entertaining part of any singing game; this version takes off in an entirely original direction after the first verse. Some accompaniments include clapping, stomping, drumming, and motions such as tapping the shoe (for *on my shoe*) or revolving one arm around the other (for *rolling home*). As memorable as it is amusing, portions of this song have been used in joke-telling, pop music, and in the study of speech development. It teaches language, counting, rhythm, and coordination. So . . . *nick-nack paddywack, sing the song below!*

COUNT ALL THE DOGS!

6 Pointers   11 Poodles   19 Rhodesian Ridgebacks   35 Basset Hounds

30 Cairn Terriers   9 English Setters   24 Alaskan Malamutes   33 West Highland White Terriers

4 German Shepherds   32 Great Danes   9 Pugs   25 Golden Retrievers

13 Cocker Spaniels*

*Don't miss Sylvia on the back jacket flap!

Including Michelangelo and Cornflake.

250 dogs appear in this book.